P9-CFD-306

FIFTH HARMONY

FAMOUS GIRL GROUP

KATIE LAJINESS

Big Buddy Books
An Imprint of Abdo Publishing
abdopublishing.com

BIG BUDDY POP BIOGRAPHIES

abdopublishing.com

Published by Abdo Publishing, a division of ABDO, PO Box 398166, Minneapolis, Minnesota 55439.
Copyright © 2018 by Abdo Consulting Group, Inc. International copyrights reserved in all countries.
No part of this book may be reproduced in any form without written permission from the publisher.
Big Buddy Books™ is a trademark and logo of Abdo Publishing.

Printed in the United States of America, North Mankato, Minnesota.
092017
012018

Cover Photo: Frazer Harrison/Getty Images.
Interior Photos: Andrew Chin/Getty Images (p. 23); Christopher Polk/Getty Images (pp. 15, 27, 29);
    Cooper Neill/Getty Images (p. 19); David Becker/Getty Images (p. 11); Imeh Akpanudosen/
    Getty Images (p. 9); Jonathan Leibson/Getty Images (p. 21); Leon Bennett/Getty Images
    (p. 17); Mark Davis/Getty Images (p. 25); Mike Windle/Getty Images (p. 13); Sonia Recchia/
    Getty Images (p. 5).

Coordinating Series Editor: Tamara L. Britton
Contributing Editor: Jill Roesler
Graphic Design: Jenny Christensen

Publisher's Cataloging-in-Publication Data

Names: Lajiness, Katie, author.
Title: Fifth Harmony / by Katie Lajiness.
Description: Minneapolis, Minnesota : Abdo Publishing, 2018. | Series: Big buddy pop biographies |
    Includes online resources and index.
Identifiers: LCCN 2017943934 | ISBN 9781532112133 (lib.bdg.) | ISBN 9781614799207 (ebook)
Subjects: LCSH: Fifth Harmony (Musical group)--Juvenile literature. | Women singers--Juvenile
    literature. | Singers--Juvenile literature. | United States--Juvenile literature.
Classification: DDC 782.421660922 [B]--dc23
LC record available at https://lccn.loc.gov/2017943934

CONTENTS

GIRL GROUP

Fifth Harmony is a popular music group. The original members were Camila Cabello, Normani Hamilton, Dinah Jane Hansen, Lauren Jauregui, and Allyson Hernandez. Fans love to see the group on popular television shows!

SNAPSHOT

NAME (left to right):	BIRTHDAY:
Camila Cabello	March 3, 1997
Normani Hamilton	May 31, 1996
Dinah Jane Hansen	June 22, 1997
Lauren Jauregui	June 27, 1996
Allyson Hernandez	July 7, 1993

ALBUMS:

7/27, Reflection, Better Together (EP)

STARTING OUT

Fifth Harmony formed in Los Angeles, California, in 2012. The group's members began as **solo** artists on the American TV show *The X Factor*. However, the show's judges thought the five girls would work better as a group.

DID YOU KNOW
The X Factor was filmed in the United States from 2011 to 2013.

WHERE IN THE WORLD?

Oregon

Idaho

Nevada

Utah

California

PACIFIC OCEAN

Los Angeles

Arizona

N
W E
S

BIG BREAK

On *The X Factor*, fans voted for their favorite acts. In 2012, Fifth Harmony took third place. Soon after, judge Simon Cowell asked the group to record an album. The group sang **cover songs** and posted videos on the website YouTube.

Fifth Harmony **released** its first **EP** in 2013 called *Better Together*. That year, the group went on tour with singer Cher Lloyd.

Fifth Harmony fans are known as Harmonizers.

In 2015, the group **released** its first album, *Reflection*. It featured the hit song "BO$$." Harmonizers loved the album. It sold more than 500,000 copies!

The next year, Fifth Harmony continued its success with a second album, *7/27*. Chart-topper "Work From Home" reached number four on the *Billboard* Hot 100. The song spent 34 weeks on the chart.

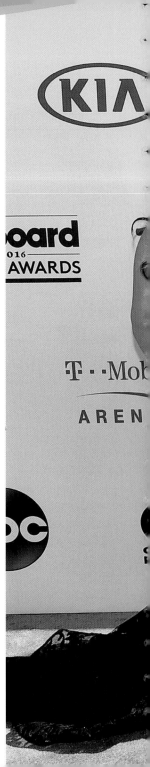

As of 2017, "Work From Home" sold 4 million digital copies!

DINAH JANE

Dinah Jane Hansen was born in Santa Ana, California, on June 22, 1997. Her parents are Milika and Gordon Hansen. Dinah is one of seven **siblings**.

From childhood, Dinah grew up singing in church. At 15, she **auditioned** for *The X Factor*. Dinah sang "If I Were a Boy" by Beyoncé. All four judges loved her **performance**.

Dinah wanted to be the voice of Moana in a Disney movie about a Polynesian princess. Sadly, she did not get the part.

LAUREN

Lauren Jauregui was born in Miami, Florida, on June 27, 1996. Her parents are Clara and Michael Jauregui. She has one brother, Chris, and one sister, Taylor. When Lauren was 16, she **auditioned** for *The X Factor*. She sang "If I Ain't Got You" by Alicia Keys.

Growing up, Lauren attended Carrollton School of the Sacred Heart. This is an all-girls school in Miami. She graduated in 2014.

NORMANI

Normani Kordei Hamilton was born in Atlanta, Georgia, on May 31, 1996. Her parents are Andrea and Derrick Hamilton. She has two half sisters, Ashlee and Arielle.

She grew up in New Orleans, Louisiana. However, her family moved to Houston, Texas, in 2005.

DID YOU KNOW?
In 2017, Normani placed third on the TV show *Dancing with the Stars*.

Normani auditioned for *The X Factor* when she was only 15 years old. She sang "Chain of Fools" by Aretha Franklin. The judges loved her singing!

CAMILA

Camila Cabello was born in Cojimar, Cuba, on March 3, 1997. Her parents are Sinuhe and Alejandro Cabello. She has a younger sister, Sofia.

When she was 15, Camila **auditioned** for *The X Factor* in North Carolina. This was her first time singing in front of an **audience**.

In 2016, Camila left Fifth Harmony. The group continued with just four members.

In 2016, Camila sang a duet with Shawn Mendes. "I Know What You Did Last Summer" sold more than 1 million digital copies.

ALLYSON

Allyson "Ally" Brooke Hernandez was born in San Antonio, Texas, on July 7, 1993. Her parents are Patricia and Jerry Hernandez. She has an older brother, Brandon. Ally **auditioned** for *The X Factor* in Austin, Texas. She sang "On My Knees" by Jaci Velasquez.

DID YOU KNOW ?

Ally was born very early. She weighed almost two pounds (1 kg) at birth. The average birth weight is more than 7 pounds (3 kg).

Ally is known for her love of social media. She once posted a video of her singing with her dog!

ON TOUR

Fifth Harmony often went on tour to sing music from its latest album. At first, the group was the opening act for famous **pop** stars. As Fifth Harmony gained popularity, the women began to **headline** their own concerts.

The 7/27 world tour was 33 shows throughout South America, North America, and Europe. The group used **social media** to tell millions of fans about their concerts.

In 2014, Fifth Harmony was the opening act for Demi Lovato's *Neon Lights* tour.

AWARD SHOWS

Fifth Harmony has won many **awards**. The group won a Radio Disney Music Award in 2014 for Breakout Artist of the Year. It also took home an MTV Video Music Award.

The group has been **nominated** for many Teen Choice Awards. It won the **Social Media** Queens and the Choice Music Group (Female) awards, among others.

Fifth Harmony took home the 2014 MTV Video Music Award for Artist to Watch. It won against Sam Smith and 5 Seconds of Summer.

Fifth Harmony has **performed** at many **award** shows. The group has been known for its strong singing and fun dance moves.

At the 2016 American Music Awards, Fifth Harmony brought the crowd to its feet. The **audience** loved the song, "That's My Girl."

Fifth Harmony performed "Work from Home" at the 2017 People's Choice Awards. That night, the group won the People's Choice Award for Favorite Group.

BUZZ

Fifth Harmony remains a popular girl group. In 2017, the group plans to **release** its third album. And, it will **perform** in Japan. Fans are excited to see what Fifth Harmony does next!

DID YOU KNOW ?

Fifth Harmony announced its first single without Camila Cabello. "Down" features rapper Gucci Mane.